THE AH SO! STORIES

of

Malcolm Phipps

(Tales of the martial arts for the young and not so young)

Illustrations by Mark Burt

BY THE SAME AUTHOR

Wild Oats in Cornwall
Uchi Deshi and the Master
The ConEquest
Little Book of Seishinkai

Dedicated to my precious Allison
and the loveable 'Beenie'

First published in 1999 by
St. Ives Printing and Publishing Co.

Text Copyright © 1999 Malcolm Phipps
Illustration Copyright © 1999 Mark Burt

ACKNOWLEDGMENTS

The author, illustrator and publishers are grateful to the following people for their help in the publication of this book:

Allison Phipps, Terry O'Neill, Patrick Mileham & Eric Harvey

CONTENTS

FOREWORD

by

Terry O'Neill 6th Dan JKA & Star of TV & Film

I have known Malcolm now for many years and his love and enthusiasm for his chosen art of Shotokan Karate is extremely infectious. I have held courses for him, and with him and all who have trained on these courses will back this statement to the hilt. He has trained in Shotokan Karate now for nearly thirty years and has developed over the years a strong and an excellent Karate Association, *SEISHINKAI SHOTOKAN KARATE INTERNATIONAL*, with many dojos throughout the world. Over these

years, he has produced champions at literally all levels, including World/European and many, many national champions but more importantly, day to day students of an extremely high level.

This, his fifth book, is a real gem, following in the traditions of his first Karate work, *'Uchi Deshi and the Master'*, which went on to become a Karate best-seller, not only in this country but in the German translation as well. He has used a handful of those original tales in this book but only because they were so important to this work. Mark Burt's superb illustrations bring these stories to life in a wonderful way and this is the second work of Malcolm's that Mark has illustrated, the first being a very funny children's novel, *'Conequest'*.

'The Ah So! Stories' is an easy-to-read and easy-to-digest philosophy on the martial arts and although a serious work, is also light-hearted in the right places and this totally describes the way Malcolm teaches. He has the superb knack of getting the very best out of his students and this book is a testament to that fact.

It is my guess, that if this book fell into the hands of people who had never put on a gi in their lives, after reading this, might just be tempted to purchase one and start training. I totally recommend this book and thoroughly enjoyed it from start to finish.

AUTHORS' NOTE

It has been my intention to make this a book for younger readers, as I believe there is very little literature available for the young student of karate, especially on the philosophy of the martial arts. I believe older students and instructors will also enjoy these stories of the East as they are timeless tales of our martial arts ancestry.

I have taken the occasional story from my first karate work, ***Uchi Deshi and the Master,*** for two reasons. First of all, these few repeated stories are of extreme importance to this work and secondly, it was by request that these stories be repeated. They are not repeated exactly and therefore hopefully will still be interesting to anyone who purchased ***Uchi Deshi and the Master.***

My sincere thanks go to my great friend and colleague, **Terry O'Neill** for agreeing to write the *Foreword* to this work and also to **Mark Burt** for the superb illustrations which have brought the stories to life.

My thanks also go to my publishers, especially **Andrew Richards**, who was so helpful in putting this work together.

My final thanks must go to my lovely wife **Allison**, who has been so very supportive and understanding whilst I was researching and writing this book.

Finally, I hope all readers, *young and old*, thoroughly enjoy these tales and understand the meanings and philosophy behind them. I believe that it is a massive part of karate-do that must not be forgotten, and I have tried my best to pass on these stories in a way that will benefit all.

'THOSE WHO KNOW'

Noritake Hagiwara was a young boy and he lived with his family in a small village about eighty miles from Tokyo. His father was the village carpenter, who worked in a large, well-equipped shed in their back garden, whilst his mother stayed at home and looked after their two year old daughter, Yoshi.

The family and indeed most of the village still lived and believed in the old traditional ways of Japan, and were not interested in the new technological age and its material trappings.

Noritake (pronounced Noritaka) was nearly eleven years old and he had one very serious passion - karate. On his tenth birthday his father had introduced him to the local teacher, a wise old gentleman who would never tell anyone his age. It was regularly guessed at by his students though, and would range from anywhere between sixty to eighty years of age. The children's class consisted of around twelve students and Noritake was the youngest. Not only was he the youngest but also the most inquisitive and the most enthusiastic. He loved the sometimes graceful, sometimes dynamic movements, but most of all he admired the Master's wisdom and patience and of course his wonderful stories. The Master seemed to have time for everyone and never had a bad word to say about any other living creature.

The class trained three times a week after school in the school hall. Weekends were devoted to the family and this was encouraged by the Master.

'Family must always come first', he had often stated.

Noritake's constant search for knowledge would often bring forth a story from the Master, usually about famous samurai, their philosophies and their ways, or of other historical heroes of the East.

It was on one such occasion, when the Master had given a telling-off to a slightly older and higher ranking student for not helping a younger one. The older student had wanted to train for his own progression and could not be bothered with teaching a beginner. All the students had witnessed this scene and wondered what the Master would do next. Noritake was no exception and so the Master sat the class down and started with the magic words,

'**Ah so!**' Every time he told a story he would always start with these same two words.

'Once, long ago in the Shaolin Temple in China, the birthplace of the martial arts, a young monk was asked by his Master to take the beginners class through a session of Kung Fu. The young monk panicked and informed the Master that he was not yet ready for such a task. The Master told him to go away and meditate and return the next day fully prepared to take the class. The young monk had an extremely restless night wondering whatever to teach the new monks. The Master had always taken these classes and was going to be a hard act to follow. The next day arrived all too quickly. The class was already assembled as the young monk arrived at the training area. He removed his sandals and made his way to the front of the class. The Master sat wisely in a corner and waved for the young monk to proceed. The silence was unnerving as the young monk took in a large gulp of air and quickly asked the class,

'Does everyone know what I am going to teach today?'

The class looked puzzled as they shook their heads and said, 'No'.

'Well there seems little point in carrying on, class is dismissed!'

The monks although a little confused, bowed and went on their way.

The Master called the young monk over to where he sat.

'That was a disgrace, whatever were you doing?'

'My humble apologies Master', he bowed deeply.

'Well this is not good enough', the Master stated, 'You will take tomorrow's lesson instead'.

The young monk bowed again and left for yet more meditation. Next day arrived and the young monk felt even worse. The class was lined-up as before, with the Master sitting quietly in the lotus position in the corner. He waved his hand in a gesture for the young monk to continue. The monk again removed his sandals and made his way to the front of the expectant class.

'Does everyone know what I shall be teaching today?' he asked.

The students were now wary to this question and, as one body, all nodded in unison,

'Yes!'

'Well if you already know there seems little point in continuing!' and with this remark he bowed and again dismissed the class. The monks slowly moved away scratching their heads, some smiling, some chatting in utter disbelief.

The Master once again severely admonished the young monk and told him that he would not escape this duty and that he would take the class again tomorrow and, indeed, everyday until he had conducted a decent and worthwhile lesson.

The young monk apologised, bowed and went on his way unhappily. Whatever would he do tomorrow? Another sleepless night followed.

The scene was exactly the same the very next day. There was the class all lined-up and ready to go, and there sat the Master in his regular position in the corner. The young monk removed his sandals and made his way to the front of the now very expectant class.

'Does everyone know what I shall be teaching today?' The question seemed somewhat familiar to the monks who looked around in utter confusion and disbelief.

Some shook their heads and said, 'No', whilst others nodded in the affirmative.

There followed an uneasy silence.

'Good! Well all those who know can teach those that don't know!'

And with this seemingly daring and stupid statement he dismissed the class and quickly made for the exit. The old Master caught him up quickly. The young monk panicked, 'Sorry Master, I am a failure to you. I will leave the temple forthwith'.

'On the contrary my friend, that is one of the best lessons I have ever witnessed'.

'How do you mean Master?'

'All those who know, can teach those that don't know, this is indeed an important and very wise lesson. One should always be ready to help others, no matter what their rank or status. Well done, you will make a fine monk'. He smiled as he dismissed the young monk with the customary bow.

The Master looked around at his class and their studious young faces.

'So you see it is very important and indeed one of life's great lessons to help those in need, whether in training or in the street. Class is now dismissed and I will see you all at the next lesson'.

'ONE STEP AT A TIME'

Noritake had been training hard for nearly four months and had just been awarded his first belt which was bright red. He had passed the examination with flying colours and felt extremely happy. As the Master was congratulating him on his fine performance Noritake asked,

'Master, how long will it take me to reach black-belt?'

The Master smiled, 'All in good time Noritake San, there is no rush'.

'Yes Master, but at a guess how long?'

'How long is a piece of bamboo?'

The young boy thought long and hard and then replied, 'There is no answer Master'.

'Exactly. Same with black-belt, there is no answer'.

The boy's expression was one of confusion, 'But you must know roughly how long Master?'

'Not at all Noritake San, you must just take one step at a time'.

Noritake still did not look totally happy about the situation and so the Master uttered his famous words, '**Ah so!** Sit down and I will try to explain'.

Noritake obeyed and the Master began.

'Imagine it is night-time. There is no moon, it is pitch black and you cannot see a hand in front of your face. You are stood on the bank of a very wide river that has to be crossed. There is a fearful current so swimming is out of the question. There are no bridges across this river for miles in either direction. There is, however, a single line of small stepping-stones neatly spaced out, reaching from one side of the river to the other and safety. You have to get across, your life depends on it. Armed only with a small torch you proceed. Now you must ask yourself three questions Noritake. Do you shine the torch on your destination on the far side of the river? Do you shine it a few stones ahead all the time? Or do you shine it only on the very next stone, first making sure you are safely stood on the stone you now occupy? The answer I hope Noritake is an obvious one, yes?'

The young boy's eyes lit up.

'Yes I see now Master, the third one is the correct answer. The stones could be thought of as the different belts in our training'.

'Indeed Noritake San, that is correct, but this also applies to life in general. Do not aim too far ahead, until your feet are firmly planted on what you have already achieved. It is much better to do things you know well than to search endlessly for more knowledge, just for the sake of it'.

Noritake nodded as the Master carried on, 'Your training will take a lifetime to perfect, there is no hurry. Remember it is better to understand a little than misunderstand a lot. So enjoy each day and each belt for what they are'.

With this final statement the Master gestured for the young boy to stand, as the lesson was now over.

Noritake bowed and thanked the Master, then went on his way looking forward to his next session with this great man.

'WINNING WITHOUT FIGHTING'

Noritake and his dear friend Hidetake, because of their serious approach to karate training, were being made fun of and generally being bullied at school. As this had gone on now for a few weeks, they thought it was time to seek advice from the Master. Before one of the evening lessons they approached him in his office.

The Master listened intently to what the two boys had to say.

'Should we fight them?' Hidetake asked.

'No, whatever you do, do not fight them for this is probably what they want'.

'But they keep on poking fun at us Master', Noritake persisted.

'Sticks and stones Noritake San. Remember the best place to hide a small mind is in a big mouth', he smiled.

'I think I will tell them that', Noritake quickly answered.

'No, this would only provoke violence and that is the last thing we wish to do. **Ah so!** Sit down boys and let me tell you about a famous samurai swordsman'.

The boys grabbed chairs and sat quietly waiting for the Master to begin.

'The true samurai was one who practised *winning without fighting* rather than the one who fought regularly, however hard and well. For if all the qualities of a true samurai were present, then there would be no necessity to fight', the Master paused for breath.
'One well-known example of this tells of a master swordsman, Tsukehara Bokuden who lived in the sixteenth century. Whilst journeying by boat on Lake Biwa he was challenged by an aggressive and tempestuous young samurai. He replied that his art consisted of neither defeating nor being defeated, but of conquering without drawing his sword. The young samurai scoffed and persisted in his challenge, so Bokuden suggested they should settle the matter on a nearby small island, to avoid causing a disturbance on the boat. When the boat drew close to the island the hot-headed samurai jumped ashore and prepared to fight. Bokuden gave his sword to the oarsman and, taking the oar, pushed the boat back on to the lake leaving the young samurai stranded. 'That is victory without the sword', Bokuden shouted to the marooned

man. The young samurai shook his fist and cursed as Bokuden calmly eased the boat across the lake'.

The boys sat with their mouths and eyes wide open.

'What a brilliant story Master', Hidetake was the first to break the silence.

'Yes, he was a great and very fair man and one to be copied, do you not agree?' The Master looked from boy to boy.
'Yes, we must follow his example and ignore these people at school', Noritake spoke for both boys as he had seen the expression on his friend's face.

'Well done boys, that is the correct attitude to take, not only for a good martial artist, but also for a decent human being'.

The boys left the Master's office with their attitudes now completely altered. No longer would they feel embarrassed or threatened by the bullies and their so-called friends at school. In fact they would feel totally the opposite.

'THE PUZZLE'

The weather was hot and humid and in this sticky and uncomfortable climate the karate lessons seemed even tougher. The Master would never make the lessons any easier because of a change in the weather and stated many times that a good student, in any subject, should train hard at all times.

It was after such a session that Noritake turned to his best friend Hidetake, a young green-belt, 'I see Katsugi San is not here again today?'

'No, I haven't seen him for a few lessons now. Do you think he has given up?'

'Maybe. It is probably too hot for him', Noritake smiled a somewhat superior smile.

'Yes, I am sure you are right. He must be mad to give it all in, he was doing so well'.

'Oh well, he is of no importance if he cannot be bothered to turn up to the Master's lessons', Noritake shrugged and started to walk toward the changing room.

'Not absolutely correct Noritake San', the Master's voice broke up the idle gossip.

Neither boy had seen him approach.

'But surely Master, only those who turn up to your lessons are of any real importance?'

'You think so do you. Then come to my office after you have showered'.

The boys both bowed and Noritake wondered what the Master had in store for him.

After a hot shower and a cool drink he entered the Master's office.

'Ah Noritake San. I want you to take this jigsaw puzzle home with you and complete it this evening'. The Master handed him a large cardboard box.

'Why a jigsaw puzzle Master?'

'This is a very special puzzle Noritake San. From it you will learn a very important lesson. The puzzle's picture is of a very senior karate teacher and you must tell me in the morning who this teacher is and what technique he is performing'.

Noritake bowed and with the cardboard box under his arm left the Master's office.

At home and in the safety and coolness of his bedroom, Noritake cleared a large table and proceeded with the puzzle. There were around two hundred pieces to the jigsaw and these were now spread evenly over the surface of the table. He methodically built up the outside square of the puzzle and worked his way carefully inward. Two hours later and the final picture was nearly complete. As he neared the finish he could easily see that the picture was of a karate person performing a side kick. But who?

To his total annoyance he could not find the last piece of the puzzle anywhere. He searched high and low, under the table and on the table. He shook the box the puzzle had come in vigorously and then searched and shook his holdall. Still nothing.
Not a sign of the final piece. The most irritating part though was that the final piece was actually the karate teacher's face. 'Damn!' He kicked the leg of the table in disgust and utter frustration as he left the room. He would have to tell the Master that either a piece had been missing when he was given the puzzle, or that he had lost the piece in question somewhere on the way home. Or perhaps he should guess who the person in the picture was and hand back the jigsaw puzzle to the Master and say nothing. No, this would be wrong and deceitful his conscience told him, he must tell the truth.

Next day and back in the Master's office Noritake explained about the missing piece.

'So what have your learnt Noritake San?'

'Always count the pieces first Master?'

'No, no', the Master smiled. 'That is not what I meant but perhaps a good idea all the same. Which piece is now the most important?'

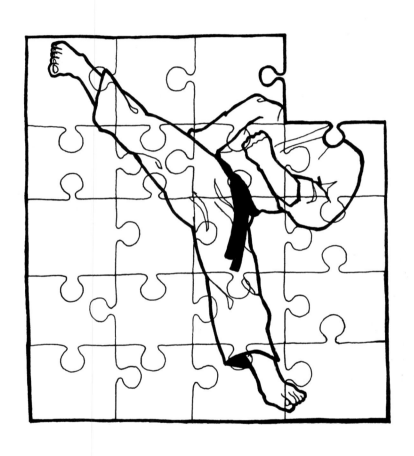

'The missing piece Master'.

'At last Noritake San and what does this convey to you about our karate class?'

The young boy pondered for a short while and eventually confessed, 'I am sorry Master, I still do not see any connection'.

'**Ah so!** Well like the missing piece in the jigsaw puzzle, the missing student is also of extreme significance. He has attained a reasonably high level in the art of karate and it is of great concern that he is missing'.

'But you can only work with those students who turn up regularly to your classes Master?'

'True Noritake San, but it is imperative to find out why our friend is not here. Has something or someone upset him? Has he not understood something? Is he ill or injured? Is his family in good health? At this moment in time, like the missing piece in the puzzle, he is of great consequence and will remain so until he reappears'.

The Master opened a drawer in his desk and produced the final piece of the jigsaw puzzle and smiled, 'I think this is what you are looking for. Do you understand now Noritake San?'

'Yes Master, but why hasn't he informed you of his whereabouts?'

'Perhaps he is too distraught or embarrassed and hasn't had time to inform us of his absence. It is important that we find out why he is missing from the class'.

'But surely the student should always go to the Master, not the other way round?' Asked Noritake.

'Not necessarily so. Sometimes roles are reversed. There are too many people in the world who expect people to come to them all the time and with this attitude, friends, families and even nations are often split apart forever'.

Noritake bowed humbly, 'Yes Master I understand now. I will call on him on my way home'.

'Good! That is the correct action for a decent human being to take. Also pass this lesson on to your good friend Hidetake San'.

'I will Master'. Noritake bowed once more to leave. As he did so his inquisitiveness got the better of him, 'By the way Master, who was the person in the picture?'

'It is of little significance Noritake San'.

Noritake's eyes looked hard at the missing piece now lying face upwards on the office table. It looked remarkably like his own Master but he didn't have the courage to ask.

'THE TIGER AND THE STONE'

Noritake frowned, as he and ten or so youngsters entered the training hall. It was all very different. No longer the shining floor. No longer the empty space where students practised their art. Instead the floor was covered with a huge tarpaulin as though the hall was about to be repainted. But the school had only been thoroughly decorated a few months ago?

Strangest of all though, the Master was nowhere to be seen and he was never late.

Noritake shook his head in bewilderment and frowned again.

All of a sudden, the outside door to the hall flew open and in strode the Master.

'Ah, good morning students'.

'Good morning Master', they all bowed as one.

'What is happening Master?' Noritake was the first to speak.

'Open the door and you will see'.

Without further ado, he swiftly opened the door and peered into the playground.

To his total astonishment, twenty or so adult students stood outside, their arms full of tiles, bricks and pine-boards.

'Hold the door open Noritake San, so they may enter'.

Noritake quickly obeyed. The students filed in one by one and placed their heavy loads in the centre of the tarpaulin. The Master could see the bewildered looks on many of the youngsters faces, 'Do not look so worried, we are not building an extension to the hall', he smiled, 'Today is breaking practice'.

Noritake's eyes lit up. He had always wanted to do this properly. Like most of the young students, he had attempted a few pathetic 'breaks' in his garden, but nothing like this. The Master walked to the centre of the hall and started to set up the equipment.

Just the one pine-board was now delicately balanced between two large stone blocks that acted as pillars. The whole thing gave the appearance of a bridge.

'Right, Noritake San. Prepare yourself to break this pine-board'.

'Yes Master', his voice slightly quivered.

He slowly strode over to where the two pillars held the dreaded pine-board. He felt so nervous and could feel everyone's eyes on just him.

'Carry on when you are ready', the Master's voice seemed to take on an effervescent tone.

'Well it's now or never', he thought to himself. He drew his fist slowly back and made a couple of dummy strikes, sizing up the task ahead. 'Hieeee!' With a powerful shout his fist fired downwards and smashed into the board. It didn't budge an inch and his fist just bounced off rather pathetically. He withdrew immediately, his cheeks now ablaze with colour. He looked around the class, embarrassment showing all over his young face.

'I am sorry Master. I do not think I can do this'.

'Rubbish Noritake San, you have a strong punch but not such a strong mind. You should be able to break one board easily. Try again'.

'Yes Master'.

The young student obeyed dutifully but again he failed, this time hurting his fist as well as his pride. The piece of wood toppled miserably to the floor, unbroken.

'Sorry Master, I just cannot do it'.

'**Ah so!** But you can Noritake San. Your mind is making your body weak. All sit down and listen'.

The students eagerly gathered round, forming a circle around their Master.

'There is a very old legend from Okinawa of a young boy and girl who were very much in love'.

The students sat quietly, their minds totally captured by the Master's introductory line.

He continued, 'One day they were out in the forest walking hand in hand, when from out of nowhere appeared a huge tiger. The boy panicked and looked for something on the forest floor to defend himself and his loved one with. But all to no avail. The tiger attacked the girl and with one foul swipe of his large razor-like paw, killed her outright. The boy was petrified, but as luck had it, the tiger ran back into the forest.

Now back in the village, the boy mourned for his loved one and vowed to kill the tiger at all costs. His whole purpose in life was to avenge the death of his beloved. And so, he took up his bow and arrows and strode out into the forest to track the deadly cat. Days passed and nothing. No sign could be seen of the tiger. Then on about the sixth day he saw what looked like the same tiger laying down asleep in the forest. Yes, he was sure it was the very same one that had taken his loved one away. He loaded up his bow and took careful aim. He loosed the arrow. It sped towards its target and penetrated the great beast deeply. The cat didn't move a muscle. It was dead. He felt elated as he strode back in triumph to his village. He told of how just one arrow was enough to kill the great beast. The villagers were so happy for him and followed him to the kill. On their arrival the head of the village called the young man over to the tiger, still lying prone with the arrow sticking out of its side. 'This is not a tiger but a striped stone that looks like a tiger'. The villagers and the young boy looked in total disbelief. Sure enough, it was exactly as the head-man of the village had said, a large striped stone. The strange thing though, was that the arrow had deeply penetrated the solid stone. 'He must be an amazing warrior to be able to pierce solid rock with an arrow', they all chattered excitedly amongst themselves, 'Show us how you did it'.

The young boy fired arrow after arrow at the striped rock, but every single time they just bounced off harmlessly. 'It is no good, I cannot do it again'. The head-man took the boy to one side, 'The reason you cannot now pierce the rock is that your motive is not strong enough. Before, you wanted so much to kill the tiger that nothing could get in your way. Your arrows could even pierce solid rock. But now there is no real motive only to show-off'. With this the boy returned to the village'.

The class sat open-mouthed.

'So you see Noritake San, if you really believe in yourself, and your motives are honourable, then there is no end to what you can achieve'.

'Yes Master'.

'Good. Now set up the pine-board again and prepare yourself to break it. Spend some time in meditation. Think on the task ahead and how you will feel when you have achieved your goal'.

'Right Master', he stood and bowed and set about rebuilding the pillars and the dreaded pine-board. This done, he knelt by them and meditated. After about a minute he arose slowly. The class sat in total apprehension. Not a sound could be heard.

Noritake sized up the wooden board, carefully measuring the distance for the immediate task now set before him.

'Hieeee!' His fist smashed into the board with a fearsome force. He withdrew and looked from the shattered board to his Master, elation beaming across his face.

He bowed deeply, 'Thank you Master'.

The Master returned the bow, 'It is amazing what the body can achieve if we truly believe in ourselves, yes? This morning Noritake San you have learnt a most powerful lesson. To know others is wisdom, to know yourself is enlightenment'.

'Yes Master. By the way Master, is your story where the saying *stone-dead* comes from?'

An artful smile crept onto his young face.

The Master laughed loudly, 'Very good. It is good to have a sense of humour and, who knows, you may even be right'.

'LOSS OF TEMPER'

The training session had been tough and the weather very humid. On top of this Noritake had had a bad day at school. Nothing seemed to go to plan. It was nearing the end of the lesson when, during some light sparring, a young brown-belt by the name of Mitsusuke caught Noritake with a punch on the nose. It wasn't very hard but it made his eyes water and gave the impression he was crying.

'I'm very sorry', Mitsusuke held out his hand in friendship.

Noritake could see one or two of the class giggling at his downfall, so he immediately flew at Mitsusuke, throwing a barrage of uncontrolled punches.

The Master caught this action out of the corner of his eye and shouted at the class to stop sparring. He made his way quickly to Noritake.

'Whatever do you think you are doing Noritake San?'

'Well he punched me hard on the nose Master'.

'Did it bleed?'

'No Master'.

'Then it couldn't have been that hard and I am sure it was an accident', the Master looked in Mitsusuke's direction.

'Yes it was Master', the young brown-belt replied, 'I tried to apologise but never really got the chance'.

'No, I understand. Class sit down'.

The students obeyed and the Master continued, ' You must never lose your temper in the martial arts, for if you do you become nothing more than a ruffian. This attitude must also follow you in life wherever you travel'.

The class listened intently.

'**Ah so!** I will tell you another story about the famous samurai swordsman, Tsukehara Bokuden. Master Bokuden, had three sons who were all trained in swordsmanship. To survey their skill in the art of the sword, he placed a cushion above a door curtain in such a way that it

would be dislodged by anyone who entered. Bokuden called his eldest son. Even before entering the room the son noticed the cushion, so he took it down and placed it where it had originally been, on a chair. Bokuden once again placed the cushion above the door curtain and called his second son. When this son entered he dislodged the cushion but caught it neatly and without fuss also replaced it on its chair. It was the third son's turn to enter. Full of confidence he entered and dislodged the cushion, but before it hit the floor he cut it in two with his sword. Master Bokuden then passed judgement on his three sons. To the eldest he presented an exquisite sword declaring him to be well-qualified in his art and worthy of carrying a sword. He recommended that his second son should train even harder and more often. But the third son was pronounced to be a disgrace to his family and should never be allowed to carry a sword'.

The Master finished his story and asked the class to stand, 'So you see it is not good or clever to lose one's temper. Remember, anger is only one letter short of danger. Now Noritake San, please apologise to Mitsusuke San for your actions'.

Noritake turned to face Mitsusuke, his cheeks a little flushed. He bowed deeply and said he was sorry. Mitsusuke returned the bow and said everything was all right.

With this the boys shook hands and from that moment on became the very best of friends.

'THE DREAM'

Noritake was having a terrible night. He tossed and turned in the heat, sweat streaming from his brow. Again the same dream. This had to be the third or fourth time, each time exactly the same. He was walking along a deserted beach with the Master. In front of them, high in the sky, Noritake's past life was being displayed in the clouds. Behind them all that could be seen were their footprints. The soothing sound of the sea was the only noise to be heard. Neither of them spoke. Noritake could not help noticing that every time something horrible or troublesome happened in his young life, only one set of footprints could be seen. When everything became rosy and going to plan, both sets of footprints would return. Why did the Master keep deserting him at his times of need? He awoke again, kicking off the thin sheet that half-covered his damp body. He must ask the Master if he knew the meaning of this dream. It was now starting to haunt him.

Next day he arrived early at the training hall. The Master sat quietly in his office reading an old book. He looked up as the door opened after the customary knock.

'Yes Noritake San, how may I help you?'

Noritake bowed and stumbled his way through his opening words, 'I do not know how to explain Master. It is rather awkward'.

'Sit down, relax and start from the beginning'.

'Well Master, I have been having this recurring dream and it has been bothering me. Each time it wakes me with a start and I am soaked in sweat. I feel a little silly coming to you with my dreams though'.

'Never underestimate the power of dreams young Noritake San. Please continue'.

Noritake told the story of the dream to the Master in every detail, leaving nothing to chance. When he eventually finished he felt a load lift from his young shoulders.

'That is it Master'.

'I see', the Master was now in deep contemplation. Eventually he spoke,

'**Ah so!** Yes I know the meaning of this dream Noritake San'.

'You do Master', he felt a sudden surge of relief.

'I will explain. In your dream, when things were going well, I was always by your side, yes?'

'Yes Master, two sets of footprints'.

'And when things got a little rough in your life, only one set of prints could be seen, true?'

'Yes, that is it Master'.

'It was then, in those troubled times Noritake San that I carried you. That was the reason for only one set of footprints'.

Young Noritake sat flabbergasted. All had been revealed by this great man. A small tear welled-up in his eyes for he knew this to be true. 'I do not know what to say Master except thank you'.

'The only thanks needed Noritake San is that you train hard and always have respect and loyalty for your elders, passing on the good ways to others you touch on your journey through life'.

'I will Master', and with this he bowed and left the Master's office, not for the first time a little wiser.

'A SUMMER LESSON'

It was mid-summer and it was hot, very hot. The forest was green and lush and the sound of the birds was all you could hear for miles. The class stood patiently in a clearing, somewhere in the centre of the vast forest, awaiting the Master's next instruction.

It was the outdoor training weekend, an event organised by the Master every summer. The students would train and literally live off the land for two long weekends each year, one in the middle of summer, the other in mid-winter. The Master had carefully explained that there was nothing better for the character and comradeship than the outdoor training sessions.

'Partner-up for light sparring practice!' he powerfully commanded.

The thirty or so students, adults as well as children, all quickly found themselves a suitable partner and stood ready for the Master's command to begin.

'Right, now change partners', the Master smiled noticing that nearly everyone had partnered their best friend.

'You will not learn very much if you keep on partnering your friend. A student needs to feel challenged, not comfortable, if he or she is to better themselves'.

The attackers moved swiftly, even on the rough terrain as they delivered their vigorous but controlled attacks. The piercing and spirited shouts from the students made the birds in the trees move swiftly to a safer distance. Defenders became attackers and attackers, defenders as the gentle sparring moved to and fro across the forest floor. On one such attack Noritake stumbled badly on a large twig and lost his balance. His partner, Hidetake, luckily enough had excellent control and stopped his blow an inch from young Noritake's nose. 'Hieeee!' His opponent's fierce shout accompanied the telling strike.

Noritake regained his composure and rubbed his now painful ankle. He grinned at his opponent who in turn smiled back. Smiles turned into chuckles, chuckles into hoots as both could see the funny side of the incident.

'What is the joke?' The Master was now by their side.

'I stumbled on a tree root Master'.

'So what is so funny about that Noritake San?'

'Er, I do not really know Master', he felt extremely awkward and somewhat stupid.

'Your mistake could have cost you your life in real combat. It is certainly no laughing matter'.

The two youngsters bowed as one and apologised.

'**Ah so!** There is an important lesson to be learnt here. Class gather round'.

The students obeyed immediately and formed a tight circle around their teacher.

'If we learn nothing else on this weekend, then so be it. What I now have to say is of extreme importance'.

The class listened intently to their Master and again the only sound to be heard was that of the birds and the odd insect.

'When you make a mistake, as our two friends here have made', he pointed in their general direction, 'do not laugh, it is a sign of weakness. The human is the only animal that laughs at its own mistakes. All other animals learn immediately from their shortcomings, they do not find them in the least bit funny. We must learn from the animal kingdom as our fathers before us and their forefathers before them and indeed the founders of the martial arts did all those many years ago. Many styles and movements in the martial arts come directly from the animal kingdom'.

The class was now completely engrossed as the Master proceeded.

'As with the animals, the student should be at one with their surroundings. Development of our minds can only be achieved when the body has been disciplined. To attain this state we should try to imitate God's creatures. All creatures, whether great or small are at one with nature. We must have the wisdom to learn their many qualities. From the crane we learn poise and balance and from the snake supreme suppleness. We can observe near perfect timing from the mongoose, whilst the praying mantis teaches us composure and speed. The tiger

teaches us tenacity and power, and the falcon, supreme patience and a lightning strike. In nature, no two elements are in conflict. Therefore if we follow the ways of nature we remove conflict from within ourselves. We discover a harmony of mind, spirit and soul in accordance with the natural flow of the universe'.

The class sat open-mouthed.

'Now do you understand?' He gazed at Noritake and Hidetake.

'It is wrong to laugh at one's mistakes. Learn not laugh! Now partner-up again'.

'Yes Master!' They bowed with deep respect. Both inwardly knew they had just learnt a very meaningful lesson and one that would stay with them for the rest of their lives.

'THREE SIGHTS'

The evening lesson was coming to an end. The Master had made the young class work extremely hard and the students were now feeling completely exhausted.

'Arms slowly up and breathe in deeply through your nose', the class silently obeyed the Master's instruction, lifting their weary arms above their heads.

'And now, slowly exhaling through your mouth, bring your arms down to your sides'.

The class repeated this exercise five times.

Noritake felt much better now both mentally and physically.

'Gather round in a small circle and be seated for today's lesson', the Master gestured for the class to sit.

They gathered round him quickly, shuffling themselves into place.

'Noritake San', the Master looked him in the eyes, 'Which is the most important day in your life?'

The young boy thought for a moment, 'The day I was born Master', he confidently replied.

'Mmmm', the Master stroked his wrinkled chin.

'And you Ryusho San, what day is to be your most momentous?' The Master now directed his question to a young brown-belt.

Ryusho quickly and rather smugly replied, 'The day I pass and receive my black-belt from you Master'.

Ryusho liked his own answer very much and was reasonably confident he would receive a satisfactory pat on the back.

'Mmmm', the Master pondered for a second and finally announced, 'Both are good answers, but not quite correct'.

Ryusho looked quickly at Noritake and Noritake reciprocated.

It was the classes turn to look smug. The Master on seeing this then asked the whole class the same question, 'What then is your most important day?'

'The day we could first talk Master?'

'The day we first started karate training Master?'

'The day we leave school and get a job Master?'

'The day we get married Master?'

Certain children let out a 'Yukkk!' at this thought.

'The day when we have our own children Master?'

'OK enough!' He lifted his hands for them to stop, a smile on his lips.

'These are all good answers, but not the one I am looking for'. He looked at them all in a fatherly fashion. 'The most important day of your lives is *today*!'

The class sent quick and furtive looks to each other not quite understanding the Master's drift. What was so good about today? Had they missed something?

He read their thoughts.

'**Ah so!** Let me explain. There are three sights in life. First, we have hindsight. This is looking back into the past. It is good to have memories, some good and some bad, but we must not live in the past. It is gone and there is nothing we can do about it. We cannot have those times again. Secondly, we have foresight or looking to the future. It is good to have plans and dreams, but we should not live in the future as nobody knows what is in store for us. We may not even be here tomorrow. So this also is a waste of time. Finally, we have insight or living for the day. We must learn to live for the moment, for, in all truthfulness, it is all we have. The past is gone, the future may not happen, so it is for today we must live. That is why it is called the *present* as it is a *gift* from God. Enjoy every minute, for time itself cannot be regained. It is a most precious commodity. I hope you all understand?'

'Yes Master', the class spoke as one with true sincerity for they all knew in their hearts that this was the very truth.

'Good. Now get the cleaning cloths and buckets and clean the hall floor'.

After every lesson the training hall was cleaned by the students and so they stood up and made for the small cupboard next to the Master's office. Buckets were filled with disinfected warm water and the cloths dampened. The class stood in a line at one end of the hall and on the command of the Master ran backwards in unison, cloths pressed firmly to the floor.

'You see', shouted the Master, 'It is a little like cleaning the floor. The most important piece is the piece you are actually cleaning, not the parts you have gone past or not yet reached. If you do this properly you will have no need to worry, for the job will have been done correctly in the first place', he strode towards his office.

He turned at the very last moment, 'Noritake San, you have missed a bit. Look there!' he pointed to a small dry patch, a wry smile appearing on his wise old face.

'THE STONE-CUTTER'

On the floor of the training hall, a black-belt in his mid-teens was practising with a friend. His movements were lightning fast and well-balanced, and he was the envy of all the younger students. From the entrance of the hall Noritake watched in awe with his friend Mitsusuke.

'I wish I was him', Noritake proclaimed to his friend, 'Look how good he is'.

'Yes, me too', Mitsusuke sighed, 'I'll never be that good'.

Unbeknown to the two boys the Master stood right behind them.

'**Ah so!** Never wish to be anyone else, just be yourself. You were placed upon this earth to be you, not someone else. Let me tell you the story of a humble stone-cutter.

Once, long ago, lived a stone-cutter. One day, whilst working hard on a large piece of rock in the sweltering heat of the summer, he saw a fine prince pass by on his horse with his servants. He looked on in envy and wished out loud that he would give anything to be that prince in all his finery, surrounded by riches and servants. Immediately there was a blinding flash and the stone-cutter found himself sat upon a horse. He was finely dressed and had many servants surrounding him. His wish had come true. Now he lived like this for a while, until one day the heat was unbearable. The sun shone so brightly it burnt his skin and made him sweat profusely. He felt extremely sticky in all his fine clothes and very uncomfortable as he sat upon his fine steed. He looked up at the sun. Now that is real power he thought, I wish I had power like that. Again there was a blinding flash and lo and behold he became the sun. It was good. He shone down and showed his immense power to everyone, scorching the fields and making everyone hot and uncomfortable.

This made him very happy until one day a large, black cloud came by and blocked out his light. The sun could not find a way through this thick cloud and he thought, now that cloud has even more power. I wish I had that power. In less than a second his wish had come true, he was now the cloud. And it was good. He sent rain and lightning in all directions, shattering trees and blowing the tiles off buildings, but one large boulder stood firm against all his fury. No matter how hard he tried he just could not move the huge rock. He sent everything against

the boulder but all to no avail. Now that power is awesome he thought, I wish I had that power and immediately, Whoosh! He became the boulder. And it was good. He stood against wind, rain, lightning and sun, indeed against absolutely everything. He felt more powerful than anything on the Earth, until one day a stone-cutter came by'.

The Master finished his story in absolute silence, eventually asking both boys if they understood its meaning.

'Yes Master', they spoke as one, 'Be yourself and be happy with what you have and who you are Master', Noritake continued.

'Exactly! Remember that for the rest of your lives, for it is the very secret of happiness. Now off you both go and get changed for today's lesson'.

'THE TURTLE AND THE SCORPION'

In the last few weeks, Noritake had been constantly bullied at school by two bigger boys, a year or so older than himself. Every time they spotted Noritake, they would run up to him, push him about, and mock and jeer him about his karate training.

One day though, one of the bullies found himself in trouble. He was on his way to school, when out of nowhere a huge dog appeared. The dog was angry and bared its teeth at the boy and one wrong move would mean certain attack.

Noritake himself was on his way to school when he witnessed the bullies plight.

'Whatever you do don't move!' shouted Noritake.

'I can't', the bully replied nervously.

Noritake slowly made his way over to where the dog stood. A ridge of hair stood up on its back, as out of the corner of its eye it noticed Noritake's silent approach.

'Good boy!' Noritake tried to sound confident. As he approached he slowly started to take off his jacket. The dog now gave Noritake its full attention. It moved stealthily towards him and now stood only a few feet away, growling menacingly, pulling back its lips and showing its large white teeth.

'When I shout, run for your life', Noritake spoke quietly to the bully, never once taking his eyes from the dog.

The dog started to move slowly closer and an attack looked imminent.

'Get ready!' Noritake whispered.

As the dog pounced Noritake deftly threw his jacket over the dog's head.

'Run!' He screamed, as he and the bully made for their lives. They jumped over a hedge and into someone's garden. Once over the hedge they looked back and saw the dog tearing Noritake's jacket to shreds.

'Be absolutely quiet', Noritake whispered as they watched the dog eventually tire of the jacket, look around and move away.

When the dog was well out of sight, Noritake and his companion came out of the garden and made their way quickly to school.

The bully was speechless and extremely embarrassed. As they parted company in the school playground he turned and said just one word, 'Thanks'.

'My pleasure', Noritake bowed and made his way to class.

That evening, just before the karate class was about to start, Noritake told the Master of his adventure that morning.

'Should I have helped him Master, after the way he has treated me and others in the last few weeks?'

'Yes, you did the right thing Noritake San, two wrongs never make a right. Did you have to think about helping him, or did it happen naturally?'

'It happened naturally Master'.

'Excellent! It has become your nature to react for the good'.

'How is that so Master, he has made my life hell lately?'

'**Ah so!** As I said Noritake San, it has become your nature. Let me explain. Long ago a turtle was sunning itself on the beach. A scorpion walked up and said, 'Will you give me a ride to the island?'

The turtle said, 'No way, you will sting me.'

The scorpion said, 'No, I promise not to sting'.

The turtle was reluctant but the scorpion pleaded and begged. Finally, the turtle gave in and let the scorpion climb on to his shell. He swam out to the island and climbed onto the shore. Just as the scorpion was getting off his back, the turtle felt the scorpion's sting sink into his soft neck. Everything started getting blurry and the turtle said, 'You promised that if I helped you , you would not sting me?'

The scorpion replied, 'I know, I am sorry. I did really try but it's in my nature to sting'.

So you see Noritake San, it has become *your* nature to act kindly.'

'I see Master'.

'Believe me young Noritake San, the world needs more of your kind and less scorpions', he smiled, bowed and turned and made his way to the training hall.

'THE SAMURAI AND THE FISHERMAN'

One day, a scruffy young lad appeared at the entrance to the karate class. His clothes were in tatters and he had an unclean appearance. The Master approached the boy and after a few moments invited him to join the class. The boy and his family were poor and had an undeservedly bad name in the local community. He was not liked at school by the other children, who poked fun at him and bullied him. The Master, in his wisdom, noticed an unpleasant feeling within the class as the scruffy young lad joined its ranks.

'Right, gather round and be seated', he commanded. The children all obeyed instantly.

'There is a bad feeling in the class tonight, is this not so?'

No-one answered.

'**Ah so!** Then let me tell you a famous samurai story.

'During the Japanese occupation of Okinawa, a young samurai took pity on a lowly fisherman and lent him some money. It was exactly a year later and the loan was due to be repaid. The fisherman did not have the money, and so when the samurai approached he ran and hid. The samurai was known for his short temper and searched for the fisherman everywhere. He searched his home and searched the small town but to no avail. Eventually he walked along the beach and by sheer chance found the fisherman hiding in a small cave. 'Where is my money fisherman?' the samurai shouted menacingly. The fisherman cowered, hiding his head in his hands. The samurai slowly drew his sword.

'Before you kill me sir, will you grant me one small request?' the fisherman pleaded.

'Why should I? I lent you money when you were poor and gave you a year to pay it back and this is how you treat me'.

'Please, just hear me out sir'.

The samurai replaced his sword in its scabbard and gave the fisherman permission to speak.

'I really am very sorry sir that I have not been able to find the money, it has been such a bad year. I have just started to learn the art of karate

though and my Master has taught us, 'If your hand goes forth, withhold your temper; if your temper goes forth, withhold your hand''.

The samurai on hearing this was astounded at the wisdom contained within this remark. 'Well it is good to see you have learnt something from your training. I will be back in exactly one years time for my money and you had better have it ready.'

He then left.

It was the middle of the night when the samurai eventually arrived at his home. He was just about to announce his return when he saw a shaft of light from under his bedroom door. He crept into the room and saw that his wife was sound asleep, but next to her he could see the outline of another person. On closer inspection his temper grew, as he realised it was another samurai. He quickly drew his sword and was about to kill the other samurai, when the fisherman's words came to him. ' If your hand goes forth, withhold your temper; if your temper goes forth, withhold your hand'.

He decided he must give the other samurai a chance to explain himself and so withdrew to the entrance of the bedroom and quietly closed the door. He then said in a loud voice, 'I have returned!' On hearing this his wife got up and opened the door. Alongside her was the samurai's mother. She had his clothes on. 'Mother, why are you wearing my clothes?' the samurai asked.
'To scare away any intruders who might think the house was unprotected', she answered.
The samurai sat down, his head in his hands and quietly meditated.

The year passed quite quickly and it was the day that the fisherman was due to repay his debt. This time though the fisherman was waiting for the samurai. He bowed deeply and said, 'Thank you for your kindness sir. I have had a good year and so here is what I owe you, plus interest'. The samurai heartily patted the fisherman on the back and said, 'You keep the money, you owe me nothing. In actual fact it is I that owe you'.

The Master finished his story in silence.

'So you see class, never judge a book by its cover'.

The class sat without movement. Their mouths were wide open and, from that moment on, the scruffy young lad became a friend of the whole class. He was never bullied again, and indeed went on to become a great master in the martial arts.

'PATIENCE'

The young Noritake approached the Master in his office.

'Master, if I train three times a week with you and then at home every single day on my own, would it be at all possible to move up the belts a little faster?'

'Why do you wish to go faster Noritake San?'

The Master had this annoying habit of answering a question with a question.

'Well, I would dearly love to be a brown or black-belt as soon as possible Master'.

'But why?' The Master answered, 'It is not the colour of the belt that makes the student, it is their attitude and enthusiasm and the way they conduct their lives. These belts will come in good time'.

'But it seems to be taking an eternity Master'.

'**Ah so!** Patience, patience Noritake San. Let me tell you another story of the famous swordsman Bokuden'.

Noritake took a seat at the Master's request and listened intently.

The Master began.

'Bokuden, in his latter years, devoted his time to teaching the way of the sword. He would purposely make the students learn patience by making them wait a long time before actually teaching them any sword technique. One such student, after being accepted did nothing but clean and cook for six months. After this time the student's patience was at an end and he asked when he would actually start to learn any swordsmanship.
He complained bitterly to Bokuden that he hadn't come to clean and cook, but to become a swordsman. Bokuden informed the student that lesson number two would start the very next day. The student left bewildered, not quite knowing what lesson one had actually been.

That night as the student lay sleeping, Bokuden crept into his room and thrashed him violently with a bamboo stick. This became the very first of many such attacks, as Bokuden would attack the young student at any

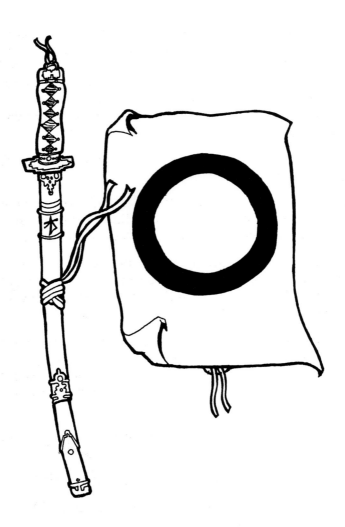

time, whether he be working or sleeping. After a few weeks the Master changed his weapon, using the flat of his sword to beat the student, showing no mercy whatsoever on these surprise attacks. This onslaught lasted for two whole years before the Master finally let the student carry a sword.

Even then the attacks still took place, but now the young student started to block and parry these onslaughts with his own sword. Eventually after many months, the student, whether asleep or at work, could sense the presence of the Master and would jump up and defend himself successfully. It was on one of these such meetings, that the Master spoke to the student for the first time since lesson number two had started long, long ago.

'Today you have become a swordsman. Come to my quarters for I have something for you'.

The student followed the Master to his house and was there presented with a beautiful Japanese sword and a certificate made out of rice paper. The only thing on the certificate was a black circle.

'The circle represents the mirror of your mind. It works best when it is uncluttered', the Master informed the student and with this gesture the student bowed and left the house of the Master forever. The student went on to become one of Japan's greatest swordsmen.

So you see Noritake San patience is a very important element in our training. All will come in time. Many people never learn patience in their whole lives, always wanting everything instantly. It is good to learn to wait, and be happy with what you have now. Keep in mind these few enlightened words'.

The Master paused before he spoke again, therefore gaining Noritake's full attention.

'Do not fear going forward slowly, fear only to stand still'.

Noritake smiled and bowed. He thanked the Master, and left his office for home.

'THE TUNNEL'

Noritake had fallen out with his best friend at school. It was over a silly, trifling matter and the argument had gone on now for weeks. Neither boy would speak to the other and, if not ignoring each other, they would be head-to-head in an argument.

Noritake was fed-up with this situation and after one karate lesson approached the Master with his problem. After listening intently to the boy's dilemma, the Master eventually spoke.

'**Ah so!** Noritake San. It is up to you to make the first move. You must prove that your training in the martial arts has been of some use to you. At this moment in time you are both stubborn and it will take wisdom on your part to heal this wound. Picture this. You stand before a long, dark and straight tunnel that you have to walk down. As you stand at the entrance and look down through the darkness, you see a pin prick of light which is the exit at the other end. Now if you stand still, or indeed turn back you achieve absolutely nothing. If you start your journey down the tunnel, for a long time it will still seem that you are getting nowhere. But as you progress further, the light becomes slightly larger and eventually after many, many steps you stride out into the light and everything is revealed. You have conquered the tunnel. Now life is often like this tunnel. If you wish to achieve anything at all in life worth doing, then you must make the first step. Remember the light will not come to you, you will have to go to it. It has been said many times that even the longest and most arduous journey started with the smallest step. If this was not so, mankind would never have accomplished anything. It is those that dare to travel down life's tunnel that overcome their problems and weaknesses.

So go to your friend and make peace with him. Be bold and take that first step and all will be well, believe me Noritake San. The stronger person is the one that apologises, not the one who harbours ill feeling'.

Young Noritake bowed and thanked the Master for his wisdom.

'I will go to him today Master'.

'That is good Noritake San, for old wounds only fester'.

And with these final words from the Master, Noritake sought out his old friend and made his peace with him.

'MIRROR IMAGE'

Noritake was slowly but surely moving up the karate belt system. He was now a purple-belt and halfway up the belt ladder from a white-belt beginner to the coveted black-belt. He was gaining proficiency in the fighting side of karate and the other children in the class could not beat him. This though had a somewhat sad side-effect, as he was slowly becoming boastful and swollen with pride. The Master caught him in the changing room boasting to his friend Mitsusuke.

'I can beat everyone in the dojo now Mitsusuke San'.

As his young friend was about to answer the Master interrupted.

'There is still someone you haven't beaten Noritake San'.

'Well of course I cannot beat you Master, but I have beaten everyone else regularly'.

'**Ah so!** Let me tell you the tale of a swordsman who also thought he could beat everyone'.

Noritake and his friend Mitsusuke sat on the changing room benches and listened to their Master.

'Again it involves our friend the master swordsman Bokuden. As I have explained earlier, in his latter years he took to teaching the art of the sword to many students. One such student became very proficient extremely quickly, and could beat everyone in the class at that time. He became swollen with pride and Bokuden had started to notice this.

One day he took him to one-side and announced that he would take him to a student he had not yet beaten. The young samurai scoffed and boasted that he had beaten everybody in the class many times. Without further ado Bokuden asked the samurai to close his eyes whilst he blindfolded him. He led him into a small building and positioned him facing the wall.

'Are you ready to meet this student?' Bokuden asked.

'Yes, show him to me now', answered the samurai.

Bokuden undid the blindfold and there stood the samurai facing himself in a long mirror.

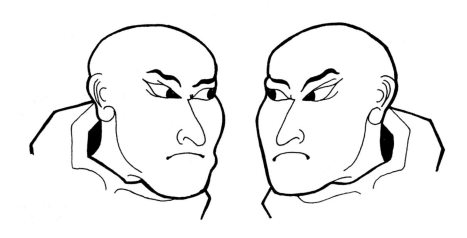

'What is the meaning of this?' He shouted.

'You are now stood before the one person you have not beaten yet - yourself! Do not be boastful, as the true martial artist is always humble, never speaking of such things. This is part of the code of Bushido - the code of the samurai'.

With this the samurai left to contemplate on Bokuden's wise words'.

'So you see Noritake San it is wrong to boast. Come over here'.

The young lad obeyed his Master and found himself now stood before a mirror like the samurai in the story. The only difference was that this mirror was misted-up with condensation from the showers.

'Wipe the mist from the mirror Noritake San'.

The boy obeyed and stared at himself in the wet mirror.

'As with the mirror Noritake San, you must wipe the mist from your eyes so you can see yourself more clearly. Everyone and everything in the universe has a purpose.

The mountain does not laugh at the river because it is lowly, nor does the river speak ill of the mountain because it cannot move'.

With this Noritake bowed and apologised to the Master and Mitsusuke for being big-headed and promised he would change his ways from this moment on.

'RICHES FROM WITHIN'

One day, the Master overheard some of the boys in the class chatting about how wonderful it must be to be rich, with no worries at all and being able to buy anything your heart desired. The Master, after listening for a while joined in with the boys conversation.

'So you think that being rich is the answer to life, yes?'

The boys pretty much all agreed that it would be very nice to be in a position where you could buy just about anything.

'Let me tell you the tale of the powerful Shogun and the peasant'. The Master sat the boys down and started his story in the usual fashion.

'**Ah so!** Once, long ago, a great and powerful Shogun lived in a fine and beautiful palace. He had everything his heart desired, great wealth, good food, a wonderful family and all that he would ever need. His secret wish though, was for the life of a peasant with no worries whatsoever. On the other side of his castle walls lived such a lowly peasant, who was extremely poor. He owned nothing except the clothes on his back and had to scratch around each day for any scraps of food for his family that the Shogun's army might leave in the dustbins outside the castle gates. He wished for the total opposite, great fortunes, nice clothes and excellent food.

One night a female Spirit came to them both in a dream. First, the Spirit visited the Shogun and asked if there was anything he desired. He immediately said he would like to be a poor man, with no responsibilities about armies and the tiresome affairs of state.

The Spirit said that next morning when he awoke he would be that poor man. 'Can I not have a quick look now?' he questioned, as he was used to getting his own way.

She then visited the poor man and he asked if he could be the Shogun, with great wealth and no worries as to where the next meal would come from. She said that he also would have his wish granted in the morning. But he too was impatient and pleaded for the Spirit to let him go now. The Spirit agreed to both men's pleadings, but said she would only give them a glimpse now and in the morning they would then become the new person.

The Shogun was taken to where the poor man lay asleep. He lay in total squalor in the clothes that he had worn during the day. Rats roamed around his little hut and the general area was filthy. The Shogun contemplated this sorry scene. The peasant was then taken to where the Shogun lived. He learnt about armies and war, riches and the protection of them. After watching for a while he also thought deeply. The Spirit bade them both goodnight and said she would return in the morning to grant their wishes.

When the Spirit did return neither the Shogun nor the peasant wanted to change their life styles. The Shogun said he could not live in such squalor and it would not be fair on his family. The peasant stated he knew nothing of armies, strategy and the protection of such great wealth.

And so with this the Spirit left both men in peace.

That very day, both the Shogun and the peasant looked at their lives in a totally different way. They both sang as they went about their daily tasks, happy with what they had and with who they were'.

The Master finished his story in total silence. He could see the boys thinking seriously about his tale.

'If it doesn't make too much sense now, it certainly will in the future', he confided, 'Now off you go and I will see you next lesson'.

'THE GARDENER'

One day, as the class was training, one of the young students asked if it were best to fight and beat an enemy, or not to fight and perhaps be made to feel foolish and look a coward in front of friends and other people.

'**Ah so!** There are many stories about the wisdom of great martial artists of the past and of how they would avoid fighting if they could. You remember the story of Bokuden on Lake Biwa'.

The class nodded in general agreement as this was one of their favourite stories.

'Well let me tell you one or two more. First, we have the story of another amazing martial artist called Fusen. Now Fusen was a most feared fighter who had never once been beaten. He was a good and humble man of many years and didn't like to boast about his amazing fighting ability. One day he was working in his garden, moving large stones around to clear the way to make a new path. As he worked a young samurai entered the garden.

'I am looking for the great fighter called Fusen', he asked the gardener.

'Why do you wish to see him?' Answered Fusen.

'I wish to fight with him, to see if what people say is true'.

'And why do you want to do that?' Fusen asked politely.

'Because I believe I can beat him', the young samurai replied cockily.

On hearing the samurai's answer, Fusen went over and picked up the largest boulder in the garden. It was absolutely huge and no man on earth should have been able to move it, let alone pick it up. The samurai, on witnessing this amazing feat, asked the gardener who he was and what martial arts status did he hold.

'Oh, I am nobody special, just one of Fusen's lowly students'.

The samurai on hearing this retreated quickly, making his excuses that he could wait no longer and how he had to be somewhere else. He secretly thought, that if this powerful gardener was only a lowly student of Fusen's, then how much more strength would his Master have?

Fusen carried on with his gardening totally unperturbed. There was a slight hint of a smile on his wise old face'.

The class enjoyed the story as the Master carried on,
'So you see wisdom is better than brute strength. It takes a real martial artist to understand this'.

'THE HORNET'

The class thoroughly enjoyed these fantastic stories of famous martial artists of long ago.

'Master, you said you would tell us one or two stories. Could we please hear another?' It was the young Noritake.

'**Ah so!** Of course Noritake San. Well the next story involves a very famous gentleman indeed, Miyamoto Musashi, the greatest swordsman in all of Japan's history.

One day he was walking along a path on his way to the next town. As he walked, three bandits were waiting to ambush him from behind a small hill. Even before he got to the hill, Musashi sensed there was trouble up ahead. He saw the three bandits looking furtively in his direction from behind a small bush on the brow of the hill. As he drew closer and literally moments before the bandits were about to attack, a hornet buzzed annoyingly around Musashi's head. Without further ado, he drew his sword and with two lightning strikes cut off the hornet's wings. The hornet fell miserably to the ground and Musashi's foot put the sad insect out of its misery. The ruffians on seeing this amazing feat stayed well hidden and let the great swordsman pass unhindered'.

The class remained silent and in awe of these great men.

'So you see', the Master's voice broke the eerie silence, 'If you can avoid trouble it is your duty to do so. This is the true code of karate and indeed all the martial arts'.

'THE BULL-FIGHT'

The class was now totally hooked. Before the Master could dismiss them they pleaded with him for just one more story. He laughed kindly at their enthusiasm.

'**Ah so!** But this must be the very last one for today'.

The class all settled down for the Master's next tale.

'Long ago, in the early nineteenth century, lived a famous Okinawan martial artist by the name of Sokon Matsumura. He was a fearsome fighter and a great favourite of the people. Now the current king, Sho Ko, had just received the present of a fine and ferocious bull from the Emperor of Japan. These were troublesome times, and the king desperately wanted to keep the peasants on his side. He therefore declared, that the great Matsumura would take on his prize bull, empty-handed, at a fair to be held in the courtyard of the great palace in one months time. Now Matsumura did not particularly want to fight this ferocious animal and set about making a plan to defeat the great beast. Eventually he came up with an idea. Each night he crept stealthily into the bull's pen, and, making sure the great beast was well tethered, would stab it in the nose with a long pin he had concealed in his tunic.

This action went on for weeks until the day of the great fair. Everyone enjoyed themselves on the different stalls but secretly were all waiting for the great fight. Eventually the time arrived. The main arena was packed solid as the bull was let loose. From the other side of the arena came Matsumura, clothed in makeshift armour and a mask. The bull snorted and pawed the ground ready to attack. Matsumura strode bravely over to where the bull was noisily preparing its assault. The great beast was steaming and building up all its strength for the first charge. All of a sudden, it caught a rather familiar scent on the air. Matsumura noticed this and with a deft flick took off his mask. The bull panicked on seeing his tormentor, turned and ran for its life. The crowd cheered loudly for their champion. The king, on seeing this, gave Matsumura the grand title of Bushi or samurai.

So you see class, cunning can also work in the avoidance of trouble and fighting'.

The class all nodded in agreement and asked if the Master would tell them another story.

'No, that is enough for today. Now off you go home to your families. They will wonder where you are'.

With this the class dismissed and talked all the way home about the great warriors, Fusen, Musashi and Matsumura.

'TO OBEY, OR NOT TO OBEY'

One day a rebellious student came from another school to train with the Master.

The Master did his utmost to make the guest student feel at home, but the boy was rude and arrogant and would not do as he was told. Every time the Master asked him to do something the boy just wouldn't and questioned the Master as to why he should.

Noritake and the rest of the class watched and waited to see what the Master would do. After about twenty minutes of the boy's utter rudeness, the Master called the class to a halt.

'**Ah so!** My friend, you do not like to obey instructions, correct?'

'I do not obey anyone', the boy replied rudely.

'Is that so', replied the Master, 'Well let us put that theory to the test. If I get you to obey me, then you must promise to behave for the rest of the class, agreed?'

'OK, agreed', the boy replied confidently.

'Good. Well let us see now', the Master stroked his chin in deep thought.

'I know, come up here to the front of the class and stand on my right'.

The boy left his place in the class and strode, somewhat cockily up to the Master.

He took his place on the right hand side of the Master.

'No, actually, stand on my left, I think it will be better', the Master asked.

The boy now shuffled his way to the other side of the Master.

'No, sorry, on the right would be best after all', the Master changed his mind again as he stroked his beard.

The boy huffed and moved to his original position to the right of the Master.

'There my friend, you have at last done as you were told. First you

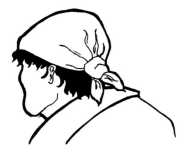

came up here at my command and then stood on the right of me, then the left and then back to the right, agreed?'

The boy woefully nodded his agreement.

'Well I suggest you return to the class and show some respect from now on'.

With this the boy took his place in the class. Not another murmur was heard out of him for the rest of the lesson.

'FLYING LESSON'

The class was out in the woods on a summers walk with the Master. It was a kind of meditation the Master liked the students to have every so often. There was no pressure of training, just watching nature at work. They studied the animals, the birds and the trees. For most of the time the class remained silent, so as to hear the natural sounds around them. Just as they approached a small stream, a rabbit raced across their path, followed swiftly by a young fox.

'Who will win the race?' The Master asked the class in general.

Nearly everyone agreed that the fox would probably win, having cunning on its side and being the more powerful animal.

The Master disagreed.

'Not necessarily so. Remember the fox is running for its dinner, the rabbit is running for its life'.

And sure enough, no sooner had the Master's words faded away, when the rabbit raced down a well concealed hole in the ground.

'There you are', the Master smiled, 'But sometimes the fox will win, especially if the rabbit is not paying attention to its surroundings. Same with life really'.

The class moved on through the woods. Noritake was now walking alongside the Master when he spotted a large duck waddling along by a small lake.

'They are such stupid and awkward creatures aren't they Master?'

'**Ah so!** You think so Noritake San. Can you fly?'

'Well, no Master', he stuttered.

'Well remember they can. They can also swim and walk and you can only do two of these three, yes?'

'I can't swim yet either Master, I am still learning', the young student admitted quietly.

'Well how can you criticise our friend the duck who can do all three quite admirably?'

'I guess I was wrong Master'.

'Indeed you were Noritake San, but do not worry. Many people expect others to be good at what they themselves can do. Everyone has a purpose in life. Some are good at one thing and some are good at other things, this is the way of the universe'.

The class moved on quietly, especially Noritake who never said another word for the rest of the journey.

'THE LEGACY'

Over the years Noritake trained hard and listened to the Master's every word.

In time, he became a good black-belt himself, as indeed did some of his colleagues in the class. Some of them went on to be the great teachers of their day and were highly respected throughout the world in their own right.

Sadly though, whilst Noritake was in his mid-twenties, the Master quietly passed away. This was a very sad day, not only for Noritake but to the art of karate and humanity in general. The words on the Master's gravestone echoed this very sentiment. The loss to Noritake was great and he felt a huge emptiness inside. He visited the Master's grave every single day, keeping it tidy in respect for all the Master had done for him. Although the Master had passed away, his words and wisdom never would. He had left a legacy for his young disciples to follow, and in time they would pass on the same message to their students.

Noritake now had his own class and he led them dutifully in the Master's way, teaching them respect, humility and etiquette. He emphasised the code of karate, that a good student should always defend the paths of truth and give one hundred percent of themselves, and that the art of karate was a never-ending quest for the perfection of one's character.

He found himself handing down the immortal tales of the famous martial artists of long ago. Stories of, Bokuden, Fusen, Musashi and 'Bushi' Matsumura were passed on to his students, as indeed they had been passed on to him.

On one visit to the Master's final resting place, Noritake could have sworn he heard the Master's voice on the wind as it brushed through the cherry blossom. Tears welled-up in his young eyes. There were only two words, but two words that Noritake had come to love and cherish, **'Ah so!'**